W9-AXH-086

DOG MAN
BRAWL OF THE WILD

WRITTEN AND ILLUSTRATED BY DAV PILKEY
AS GEORGE BEARD AND HAROLD HUTCHINS
WITH COLOR BY JOSE GARIBALDI

AN IMPRINT OF

FOR LIZETTE SERRANO
THANK YOU FOR YOUR STRENGTH, COMPASSION, AND DEVOTION TO LIBRARIES AND KIDS

Library of Congress Control Number 2018945989

978-1-338-74108-7 (POB)
978-1-338-29092-9 (Library)

12 11 10 9 8 7 6 23 24 25 26 27

Printed in China 62
This edition first printing, August 2021

Edited by Ken Geist
Book design by Dav Pilkey and Phil Falco
Color by Jose Garibaldi
Color flatting by Aaron Polk
Creative Director: Phil Falco
Publisher: David Saylor

CHAPTERS

DOG MAN
Behind the Profundity

Wazzup, Rovers? It's your old pals George and Harold.
`Sup?

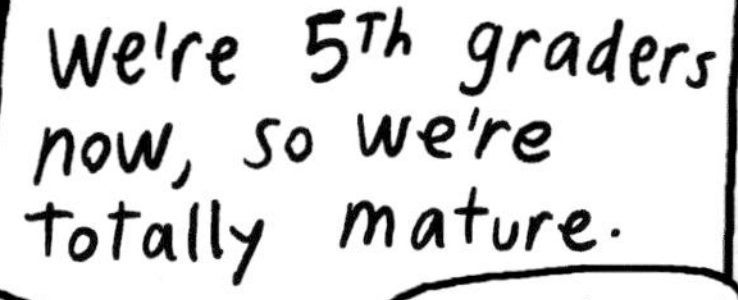

We're 5th graders now, so we're totally mature.
And deep!

People often ask us, "Sirs, do you ever miss those childhood days of Laughter and merriment?"

ALas, while we Look back fondly upon our caLLow Youths...
...We know we can never return.

For we are too deep. And too mature.
So true. So true!!!

As a very wise man* once said...
* Harold

"Enlightenment is not merely volition...

...but duty!"
Snork!

What?
You said "Butt doodie!"

HA HA HA HA HA HA HA HA HA HA

Anyhoo, we've been reading this really awesome book Lately...
The Call of the Wild
Jack London
The Call of the Wild
Jack London

...and it inspired us to write a NEW Dog Man Novel!!!

So Get ready for another Epic tale of Glorious Ginormity!!!

But First...
... a recap of our story thus Far.
Turn the page...

One time there was a cop and a police dog...

...Who got hurt in an explosion!

KA-BLAM!

They were rushed to the hospital...

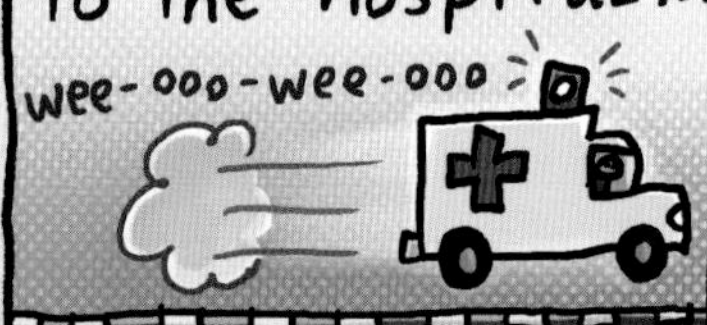

... Where the doctor had very sad news:

But then, the nurse lady got a cool idea.

Hey!

And soon, a new crime-fighting sensation was unleashed.
HOORAY FOR DOG MAN!!!
Dog Man has three awesome allies:
Sarah (very smart)
Zuzu (very brave)
Chief
Chief (very "chiefy")
... and one sinister enemy.
Peter (very evil)

But Petey's evil heart is beginning to change...

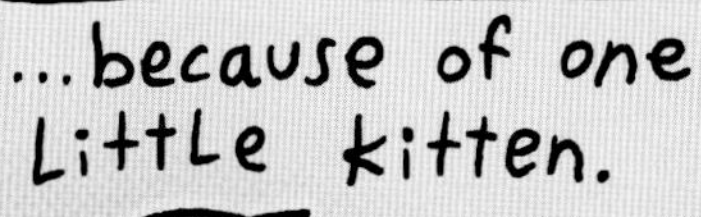
...because of one little kitten.

Li'l Petey (very good-hearted)

Li'l Petey lives with Dog Man...

DOG MAN

...and their Re-markable Robot Pal, 80-HD.

Most of the time, they're a Family...

...but sometimes, they're Superheroes.

And when we last saw them, they'd been shrunk to the size of **ACTUAL FLEAS!**

They could be hiding **ANYWHERE!**

scratch
scratch
scratch
scratch
scratch
scratch
scratch

Chapter 1

by George Beard and Harold Hutchins

Special Delivery for Chief!!!
Special Delivery for chief!!!
Special Delivery

chief
HEY, CHIEF!!!
chief

Hey, Chief! You got a special, uh....
special delivery
chief

YOU BETTER KNOCK next Time ya come into MY OFFICE!
chief

We were doing important cop STUFF!!!
chief

Gimme That!!!
chief
Special delivery
Swipe

NOW SCRAM!
Sorry, chief!
chief

AND DON'T SLAM the ---
chief
SLAM!

door.
chief

HEY!!!
chief
special delivery

GiMME ThAT!
chief
Special Delivery

LeT GO oF This RiGHT NOW!!
chief
Special delivery

InTRODUCinG
FLiP

STEP 1.
First, place your left hand inside the dotted lines marked "Left hand here." Hold the book open *FLAT*!

STEP 2:
Grasp the right-hand page with your thumb and index finger (inside the dotted lines marked "Right Thumb Here").

STEP 3:
Now *quickly* flip the right-hand page back and forth until the picture appears to be *animated*.

(For extra fun, try adding your own sound-effects!)

Remember,

while you are flipping,
be sure you can see
the image on page 19
AND the image on page 21.

If you flip quickly,
the two pictures will
start to look like
one **ANIMATED** cartoon!

Don't forget to
add your own
sound-effects!

Left
hand here.

Right Thumb here.

Chief
Special Delivery
Chief
Special Delivery
Chief
Special Delivery

chief
Special Delivery

RiP!

chief
Special Delivery
munch
munch
munch

Chief!!! What happened???
chief

I GOT a Very SPECIAL Letter And DOG MAN DESTROYED IT!
Special delivery

munch
munch
What's it say, Chief?
Hey! It's from Yolay Caprese!!!
chew
chew
chew
Yolay Caprese
39 Glamorous Rd.
Hollywood, CA.
Dear Chief,
Ciao from Hollywood!
We finally finished
making the Dog Man
Movie. Enclosed
are twenty tickets
to the red-carpet
Premiere. See ya
there!
Your pal,
Yolay Caprese

But where are the tickets?
chief
special delivery

They must have been in the bottom of the envelope!!!
chief
chew
chew
chew

chief
GULP

chief

DOG MAN!!!!!
chief

Meanwhile...
Cat Jail

Hiya, Petey! what'cha doin'?
GOOD CHART

Leave me alone, Big Jim!!!
Aw, come on...

... tell me!!!

Well, I'm trying to be good, so I made this chart to track my progress.
GOOD CHART

How long have you been good?
GOOD Chart
Let's see... thirteen, fourteen, fifteen...

Hey, do ya wanna hear about the weird dream I had last night?

No!

OK, So I dreamed I was eating this really, really, really big marshmallow.

It was so tender and fluffy and delicious...

...And Then, when I woke up, my pillow was gone!
SLap!

A-A-A-A-

A-CHOOOO!

Hey, Look--- feathers!

GET OUT OF HERE, BIG JIM!

I SAID I WAS TRYING TO BE GOOD, NOT NICE!

There's A DiFFerence!!!

I think.

GOOD CHART

GOOD
RIP
CHART

I'm a bad cat.
I can't even B
good 4 seven-
teen minutes
on my own.

Chapter 2

Meanwhile...
DOG Man
♫ Supa Buddies...

...We're bustin' up crime in your neighborhood!!!

Supa Buddies...

...We ain't too perfect but we're awfully good!

Supa Buddies, ♫ Here we come!

EviLdoers Better Run!!!

We fight for freedom – that's our duty...

... So everybody shake your booty!

Oooooooooooh, Baby baby baby shake your big, big booty...

... nowwwww!!!

Oh, hi, 80-HD!

I made some adjustments to my kitty scooter.

Now it's a **Cat HOG**!!!

What have you been working on?
Flip Flop Flip Flop Flip

Did'ja finally finish building that super computer?

Aw, **COOL**!!! You did it!!!
Supa 'puter
Flip Flop Flip Flop

Sweeeet!

Hey, 'Puter! what's up?

YOU HAVE ONE NEW MESSAGE.

Hey! It's from my Papa!

Dear Li'l
I'm sorry
C U toda

I'm
I ca
goo
tee
on

C'mon, 80-HD! Papa needs our help!!!
SUPA-PUTER

First AiD Kit

No, he's not hurt. It's **worse**!!!

He's discouraged!

Dog Man

Meanwhile...
COPS

Gee, thanks, YoLay! We can't wait!!! Bye-Bye!
chief

Well, Dog Man, it all worked out!!!
chief
click

YoLay said she'll send us twenty **NEW** Tickets!
chief

She said the movie will be Animated with **CLAY!!!**

What? You've never heard of claymation?
chief

C'mon. I'LL Teach ya all about it!
chief

First, you get some cLay...
chief
cLay

Then you moosh it around...
chief

... till you make a Little figure.
chief

Then you set it down...
chief

... and take a photo of it.
chief

Let me turn my camera on and...
chief

...Hey!!!
chief

Where did it go?
chief

chief

I guess I'll have to make a new one!!!
chief

OK, Then you just take a picture...
chief

...of the-
HEY!
chief

chief

chief

It's a mystery!
chief

Let's try This again!
chief

OKay.
chief
chief
Chief

OKay, So you take Your camera and...
Chief
HEY!
chief

Hey! You're not building a giant Robotic bumble-bee, are you?

Oh good! That's a relief!!!

Well, come with me. You've got visitors.
Who?

A kitten and a robot shaped like a bowling ball.
AW, MAN!

And so...
Hey, kid.

What's wrong, Papa?

Look, Kid, I just can't do it. I can't be good.

I tried. I really tried.

But I'm bad. I'm a bad cat.

Papa, you can't give up so easy!

Look, you're just a kid. You don't understand.

Some folks are good --- like <u>you</u>!

...and some folks are bad--- like me.

It's pointless to try to change.

It's pointless to give up, Papa.

Papa?

Goodbye, kid.

Papa, No!

Take him home, 80-HD!

This is for the best, kid.
Papa, NO!
EXIT

TAKE HIM HOME, 80-HD!
Papa.

EXIT

PAPA!
Exit

And so...
FLip FLop FLip FLop FLip FLop FLip FLop FLip FLop FLip

Left hand here.

Right Thumb here.

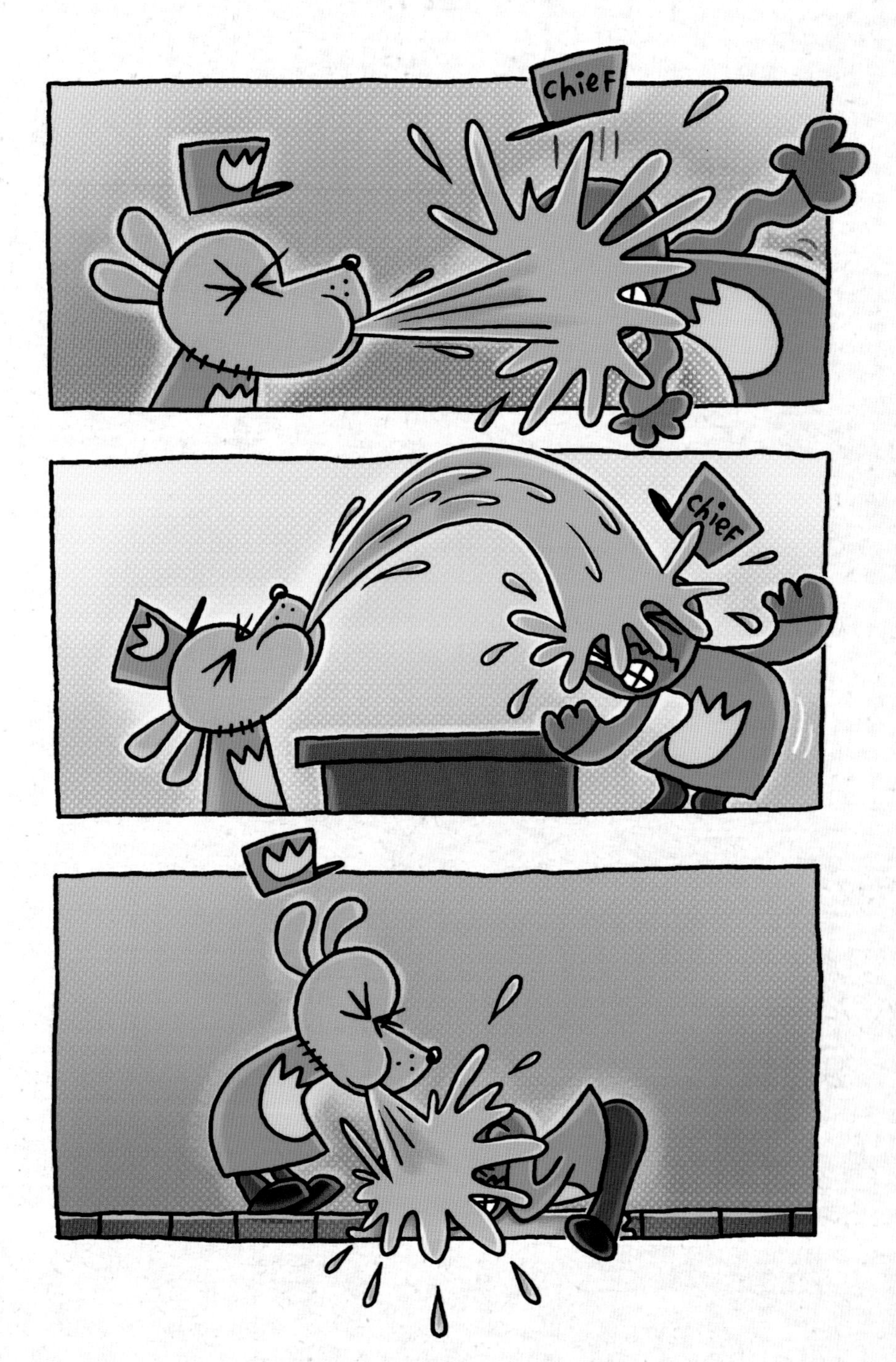
CHIEF
CHIEF

chief

chief

GET OUT OF HERE NOW!

COPS

Hey, Dog Man!
FLIP FLOP FLIP FLOP FLIP

Did ya have a sad day, too?

Don't worry.

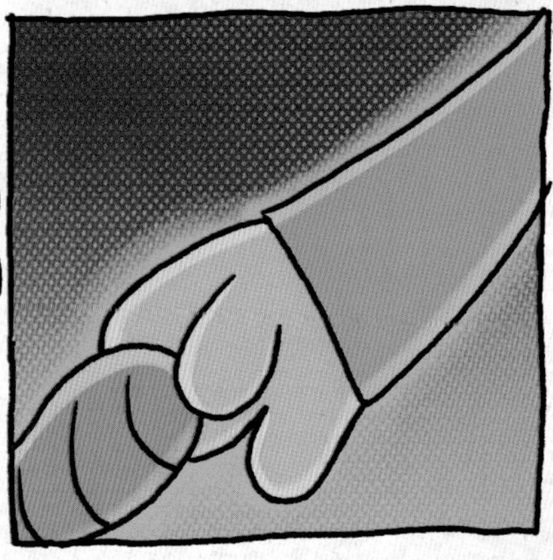

At Least things can't get any worse!!!
FLIP FLOP FLIP FLOP FLIP FLOP FLIP

Chapter 3

Things Get Worse!

By George Beard and Harold Hutchins

The city sleeps beneath the icy stars. Every soul entranced by dreams—
except for the assiduous insects.

The fluttering moths swoop in the street-lights...

...The crickets sing their soulful serenade...
chirp
chirp
chirp

...And down on the sidewalk, three flagitious fleas embark on a sinister assignment.
We're NOT fleas!

...when we teamed up against Petey and his giant robot?
Oh yeah!

Behold: the shrink ray that caused all of our problems!

Gee, I can't believe somebody just left it Lying there!
That's irresponsible!

JUST PICK IT UP AND WALK, bubs!

But it's HEAVY!!!
Don't be ridiculous! It's not heavy at all!!!

I'm SO tired!!!
Where are we going, Piggy?

We're already here!!!
CAUTION-DO NOT CROSS
POLICE LINE-DO NOT CROSS

Boing
Boing

Now aim the Shrink ray up at Petey's Giant Robot!!!

OOH--- can we press the button?
NO!!!
I did all of the work...

...So I'm Pressing the button!!!

ZAP!

CAUTION-DO NOT CROSS
POLICE LINE-DO NOT CROSS

TERRIFIC! It's not a Giant anymore!!!
OT CROSS
ICE LINE-DO NOT CROSS

Now Throw me up there!

Okay, Piggy!

SWOOOOOSH

CROSS
ICE LINE-

HAW HAW HAW!!! Now Let's get this Party STARTED!!!

The next morning...
DOG Man

Sleepy Kitty

Yawn.
Sleepy Kitty

Good morning, 80-HD!

G'morning, DOG Man!

Hey, what's this?

WHOA! Look at all of that moolah!!!
sniff
sniff
sniff

There must be a million dollars and ninety-one cents in there.

Boy, the tooth Fairy's really steppin' it up!

Hey, wait a minute...

Did you lose a tooth?

Did you???

This money doesn't belong to us.

C'mon, fellas, we gotta take this money to the cops!

FLIP FLOP FLIP

Meanwhile...
Good morning, I'm Sarah Hatoff with a breaking news story.
TV

Hey, Cops! You'll never guess what we just found!

You can't arrest Dog Man without any evidence!!!

That's a Coincidence!

And this broken window is in the shape of Dog Man!
FRANK'S BANK

That's just Circumstantial!

And check out this Photo from the security camera!

Uh-oh!

You were busy last night, weren't you?

Robbing banks... breaking into stores...

Wait'll Chief finds out what a bad doggy you've been!

Let's go, bub!!!

RUFF RUFF
RUFF
RUFF
FLIP FLOP FLIP FLOP

HEY, Quit kickin' me!!!
And You Stop that Barking!!!
RUFF
RUFF
RUFF

Stand down, 80-HD!

And you stop, too, Li'l Petey.

But Dog Man is innocent!!!!!

I Know. But if we're going to save him...

...We need to find another way.

Chapter 4

A Buncha Stuff That Happened Next

Court House
Prisoners

Stay in this cell until it's time for your trial!
Prisoners

PRisoners
SLAM

I always Knew he'd come to no good!
Me too!

Let's Face it--- He's a MiSFiT!!!
I agree!

He's not like any other cop I know.
So true.

You'll never be a REAL MAN...

'cuz You're too much of a DOG!

HA HA HA HA HA
Prisone

Poor Dog Man was desperate...
Prisoners

Dig DiG Dig DiG
... and desperate folks do desperate things.

Dig DiG DiG

DiG Dig DiG Dig Dig

Dig DiG DiG DiG

chief
POP!

I'm so PROUD of you, DOG Man!
chief
Dog Man, you ALWAYS Do the right thing!
You're the BRAVEST Dog Man I ever knew!
You NEVER run away when things get Tough!

chief
Hi, DOG Man.

I came as soon as I heard the news.
chief

Look, your trial is in five minutes...

...But I don't want you to worry!!!
chief

Everything is going to be fine. I Promise.
chief

Five Minutes Later

GUILTY!!!
chief
BAM

I sentence You to Fourteen Dog years of Hard Labor!!!

BUT, Judge...
chief

BUT, WArden...
chief
DOG JaiL

chief
Dog JaiL
NOOOOO!!!

Meanwhile...
Dog Man

Hey, 'Puter!
'Sup?
Supa 'puter

What can ya tell us About crimes and Stuff?

There were two robberies last night...

A costume shop was robbed, and then a bank.
'puter

The following items were stolen from the costume shop:

Perhaps this footage from our security cameras will be helpful.

3

3:06 AM

Sleepy Kitty
3:07 AM

Sleepy Kitty
3:07 AM

3:07 AM

Sleepy Kitty
3:08 AM

OH, NO! This is worse than I imagined!!!
'puter

We've got to save Dog Man, **AND** stop his impostor!!!

And also cheer up my Papa. He's sad!!!

Let's GO!!!

Clap
Clap

RRRRRRR
DOG Man

FWOOOOOSH!!!
DOG Man
BUBUBUBUBUBUBUBU!!!

Hey! You're Yolay Caprese, the world's greatest actress!

Guard

Sì*

* Italian for: Yo! What up?

* Italian for: You Betcha!

Do you remember me?
Guard

Aren't you the guy who kept falling into that hole?
Guard

Yeah, but it wasn't my fault!
Guard

It was that loser, DOG Man!
Guard

He's digging holes **Everywhere!!!**
Guard

But when I get my hands on him...
Guard

...He's gonna wish he was NEVER Born!
Guard

Do You hear that, Ya Stink Bubble?

Ya Cheese-nosed Oatmeal Cookie!

Ya WAFFLE-Toothed Gorilla Patty!!!
Guard

Ya raisin-Sniffin' Lemon Licker!!!
Guard

Ya Giggle-Juiced Tape Dispenser!!

WHOA!!!

KLUNK

Meanwhile...
FLip FLoP FLip FLoP FLip FLoP FLip FLoP FLip FLoP FLip FLoP
...But, Judge!!!

We have evidence that **Proves** Dog Man is **Innocent!**

It's too Late. My decision is **Final!**

* Italian for: "My Peeps!!!"

Chapter 5

Dog Jail Blues

By George and Harold

Meanwhile...
Dog Jail

DOG JaiL
Dog JaiL
Welcome to your new home, DoG Man!

You won't need this collar in here...
CLick

...because NOBODY EVER LEAVES This PLACE!

Meet your fellow inmates!

GRRRRRRRRR!!!

It looks like you don't fit in very well with the dogs.

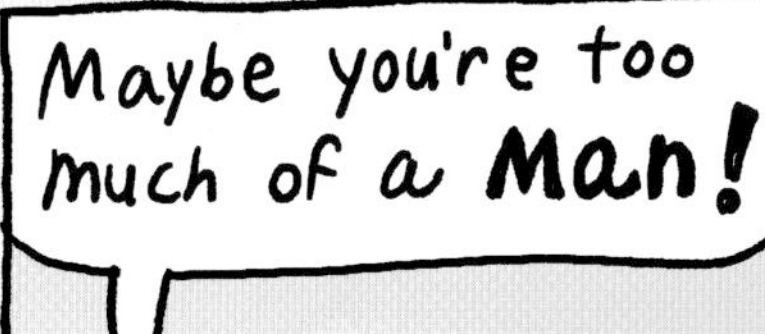
Maybe you're too much of a Man!

HAW HAW HAW HAW HAW HAW!

Oh well, you better get some rest. We've got a Tough night ahead of us.

You guys rescue Dog Man...

... and we'll catch the crook!!!

LET'S GO SAVE THE WORLD!

Hey, 80-HD, I think I have a plan!!!

whisper
whisper
whisper

Ready?

Li'l Petey and 80-HD
ARE GO!!!

BUBUBUBUBUBUBUBUFWOOOOOSH!

Cat
Jail
BZZZZZMMM

SSSSSSSHHH!!!
COPS

Meanwhile...

To: Papa
From: me

EVIL PLOT
1. escape from Jail
2. Attack city.
3. Loot.
4. Establish Supreme rulership of earth.

Hi, Papa!
Kid!

AW, COOL! Did you make that bee?
Yeah.

Can I ride on it?
No.

Why?
Because it doesn't work!

Why?
I don't know.

My blueprints are flawless!

Hmmm.

This part should be centimeters, not millimeters.

...And you forgot to carry the two.

...And you need filters on those air ducts or they'll clog the fans.

ALRIGHT, MR. SMARTY-PANTS!

I guess I'll make some adjustments!
I'll help!

Why are you helping me? You KNOW I'm the bad guy, right?

No, You're not!
Yes, I AM!!!

No, you're not.
YES, I AM!!!

No, You're not!!!
YES, I AM!

Nuh-uh!
YEAh-huh!

Nuh-uh!
YEAh-Huh!

Nuh-uh!
YEAH-HUH!!!

Hey, Papa, do ya wanna hear a Joke?

NO!!! AND DON'T CHANGE The SubjecT!

Okay. What do ya get when you cross a chicken...

...with a monkey?

I don't know. What do you get?

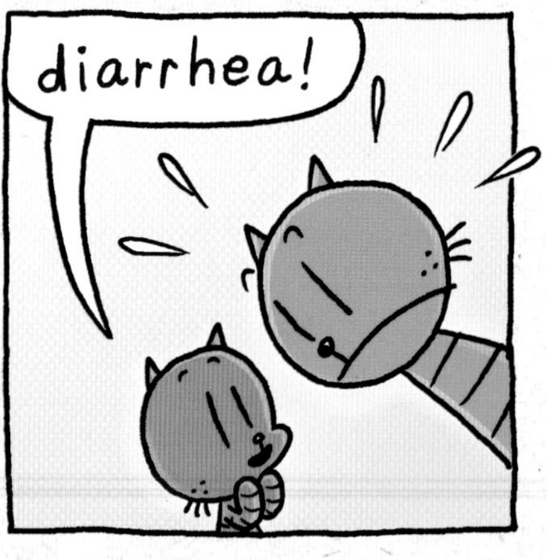
diarrhea!

Ha Ha
Ha
Ha Ha
Ha

Ha Ha
Ha Ha
Ha
Ha Ha
Ha

Ha
Ha
Ha
Ha
Ha

THAT DOESN'T EVEN MAKE SENSE!!!
Ha
Ha
Ha

And that WASN'T a joke. That was a Riddle!
Ha Ha
Ha

It's NOT FUNNY!
Ha
Ha
Ha
Ha

Meanwhile...

OK, DOG Man! Up and at 'em!!!!!

It's time to pull my dogsled to the top of the mountain...

...but don't worry. It's only 80 miles!!!

You see, I've come up with a very sneaky Scheme!
CLICK

Once a week, I collect all the dog Poop from the jail...
DOG POOP

...and then you guys pull it up the mountain...

...To this Fertilizer factory at the top!
MAP
40 Miles
Dookie BROThers' Tree Fertilizer Factory
DOG JAIL

Then I sell it and Keep all the money for myself!!!!

NOW MUSH!!!
DOG POOP

He's a MISFIT!

You'll never be a REAL MAN!!!

You don't fit in very well...

...You're too much of a MAN!
You're too much of a DOG!

Chapter 6

Even MORE STUFF HAPPENS!

By George Beard and Harold Hutchins

Meanwhile...
COPS

Knock Knock
Knock
CHIEF
Come in.

80-HD!
Chief
FLIP FLOP FLIP FLOP

Dog Man is in BIG Trouble!!!
Chief

Chief

Chief

chief

chief

CRACK!
chief

I DON'T KNOW WHAT YOU'RE TRYING TO SAY!

chief
Art Supplies
chief
Art Supplies
chief
crayons
DRAW
Draw
Draw
fold
fold
fold
chief
chief
Staple
staple
Staple

So you want me to help ya bust Dog Man out of Jail?
Chief

That's ILLegal! That's Dangerous! That's Irresponsible!

Chief

It goes against every Law I've Sworn to uphold!!!
Chief

Let's DO it!!!
Chief
FLip FLOP FLip FLOP FLip

Oh boy, This is gonna be GREAT!!!
Chief
COPS

Meanwhile...
Cat Jail
Hey, Papa!

Do ya wanna hear another Joke?

NO, I DO NOT!!

Aw, come on. It's a SUPA good one!

NO!!! I'm getting tired of your made-up Jokes!!!

This one's not made up. I got it from a book!

I SAID NO!

OK. What did Batman get for Valentine's Day?

IT BETTER NOT BE DIARRHEA!!!

It isn't! Seriously. He didn't get diarrhea.

Alright, then.

Hmmm...

Let me think...

Okay. I give up. What did he get?

Diarrhea.

Ha Ha
Ha
Ha Ha
Ha Ha
Ha

THAT JOKE DIDN'T COME FROM A BOOK!
Ha Ha
Ha Ha
Ha
HA Ha Ha

Meanwhile...

BONK

KLUNK
DANGER
I helped!!!

Chapter 7

Girl Power!

By George and Harold

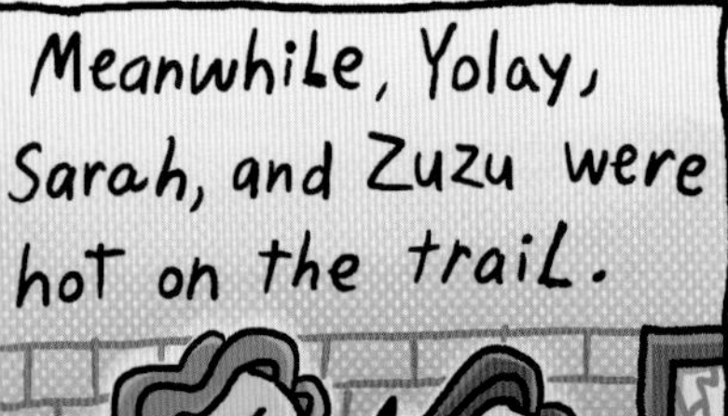

Meanwhile, Yolay, Sarah, and Zuzu were hot on the trail.

My investigative reporting skills led us to the seedy side of the city...

...And Zuzu's Sniffing skills are picking up the scent...
Sniff
Sniff Sniff

Now, I Shall use my Charismatic "People Skills" to get clues!

Watch this!!!

Hey, Booger Breath!

Do you have any clues about a Dog-headed crook?

MAYbe I DO, MAYbe I Don'T!

Grab!

WHAM

OOH--- You're in for A WORLd oF PAIN, MISSY!
Let's go!!!

The MAIN EVENT:
YOLAY CAPRESE
VS.
BOOGER BREATH
DING- DING- DING!!!
Left
hand here.

Right
Thumb
here.

Have ya had enough?

OR are ya ThirsTy for MORE???

OKAY!!! OKAY!!!

I saw that DOG-headed crook!!!

He was robbing That Living Spray FacTory OutLet over There!

M-M-May I go now, please?

Say "Pretty Please!"
Pretty Please?

What? No Sugar?

Pretty Please with Sugar on Top And Whipped Cream And Those Little chocolate sprinkles! WAAAAAAAAAAAH!!!

Wow! Those were Some impressive "People Skills," YoLay!
I Know, Right?

Chapter 8

Help is on the Way

COPS
So they're closed, eh?
DOG JAIL
CLOSED
We'll be back soon!

chief
Cops
I had a feeling that warden was up to no Good!!!

Let's follow those dogsled tracks!!!
COPS

chief
COPS

MEANWHILE

Are you done installing those filters?
Yeah.

Well quit goofing around and get out of There!!!
OK.

Hey, Papa, Y'wanna hear another Joke?

NO, I DON'T!!!
AW, come on!!!

You SAID You were gonna help me!!!
I AM!

MAking up Jokes is NOT HeLpfuL!

This one's not made up. It's from a TV show!

NO!!!

Okay. What do you call a worm from King Arthur's court?

Hmmmm...

A "Knight" crawler?
No.

Sir Squirms-a-Lot?
Nope!

Okay, I give up. What do you call him?

Diarrhea!

Ha
Ha Ha
Ha
Ha
Ha

Ha
Ha Ha
Ha

Ha
Ha
Ha
Ha Ha

WHAT iS WRONG WiTh YOU??
Cat
Jail

Meanwhile...
There he is!
chief
COPS
Dog Poop

Dog Poop
WHOA!

So! You've come to rescue your little friend, eh???
Dog Poop

Well, You're too Late!!!

Just look at him!
DOG POOP

He's **Changed!!!**

His spirit is **Broken!**

His will has been **CRUSHED!!!**

He'll **Never** be the **SAME** again!

But don't feeL bad...
DOG POOP

...You see, Dog Man's not really a Dog **OR** a man!

He's a **MISFIT!!**

Even the other dogs don't like him!

You should have seen them all growL at him when he got here!!!
DOG POOP

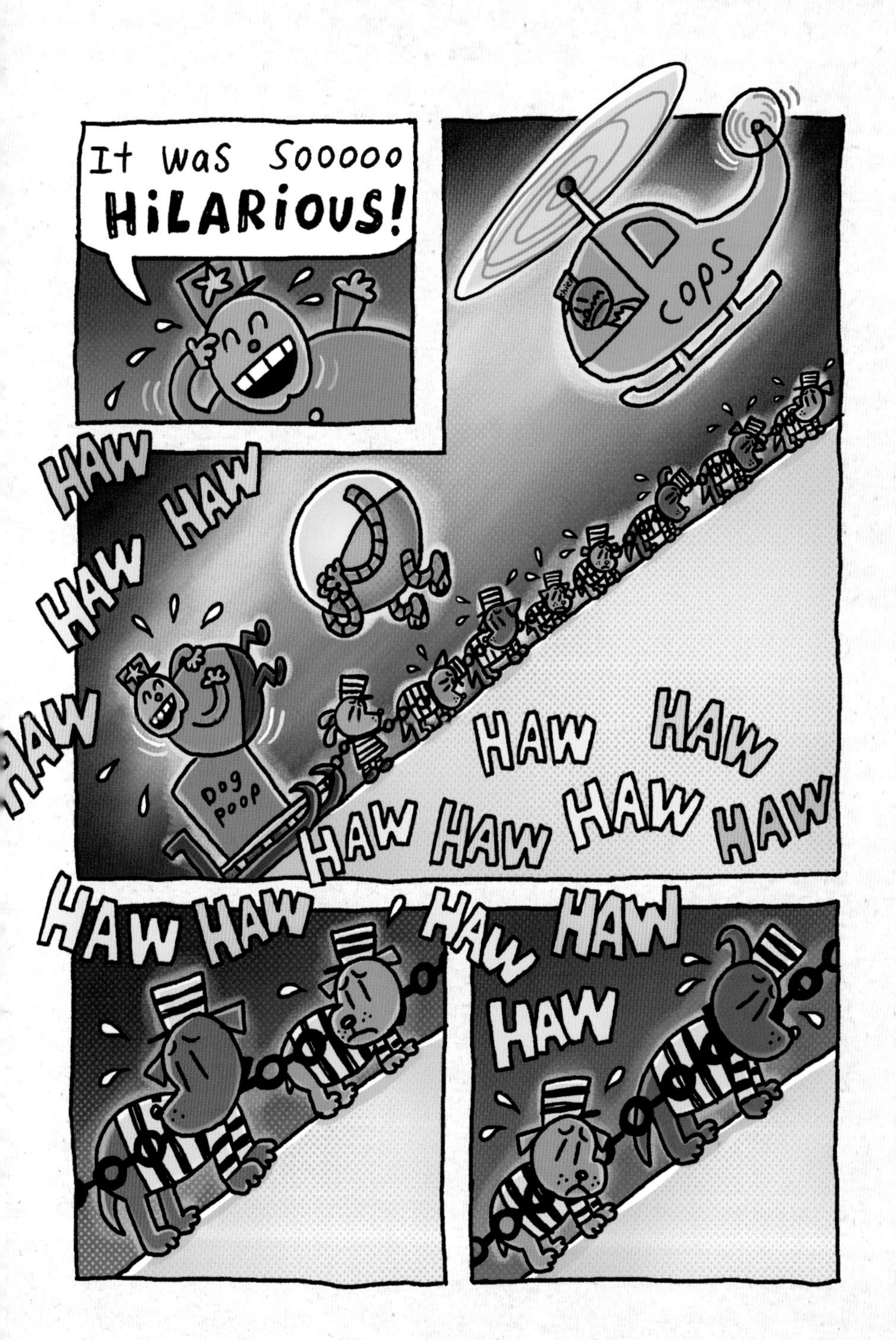
It was Sooooo HiLARIOUS!
COPS
Chief
HAW
HAW
HAW
HAW
Dog poop
HAW HAW
HAW HAW HAW HAW
HAW HAW
HAW HAW
HAW
HAW

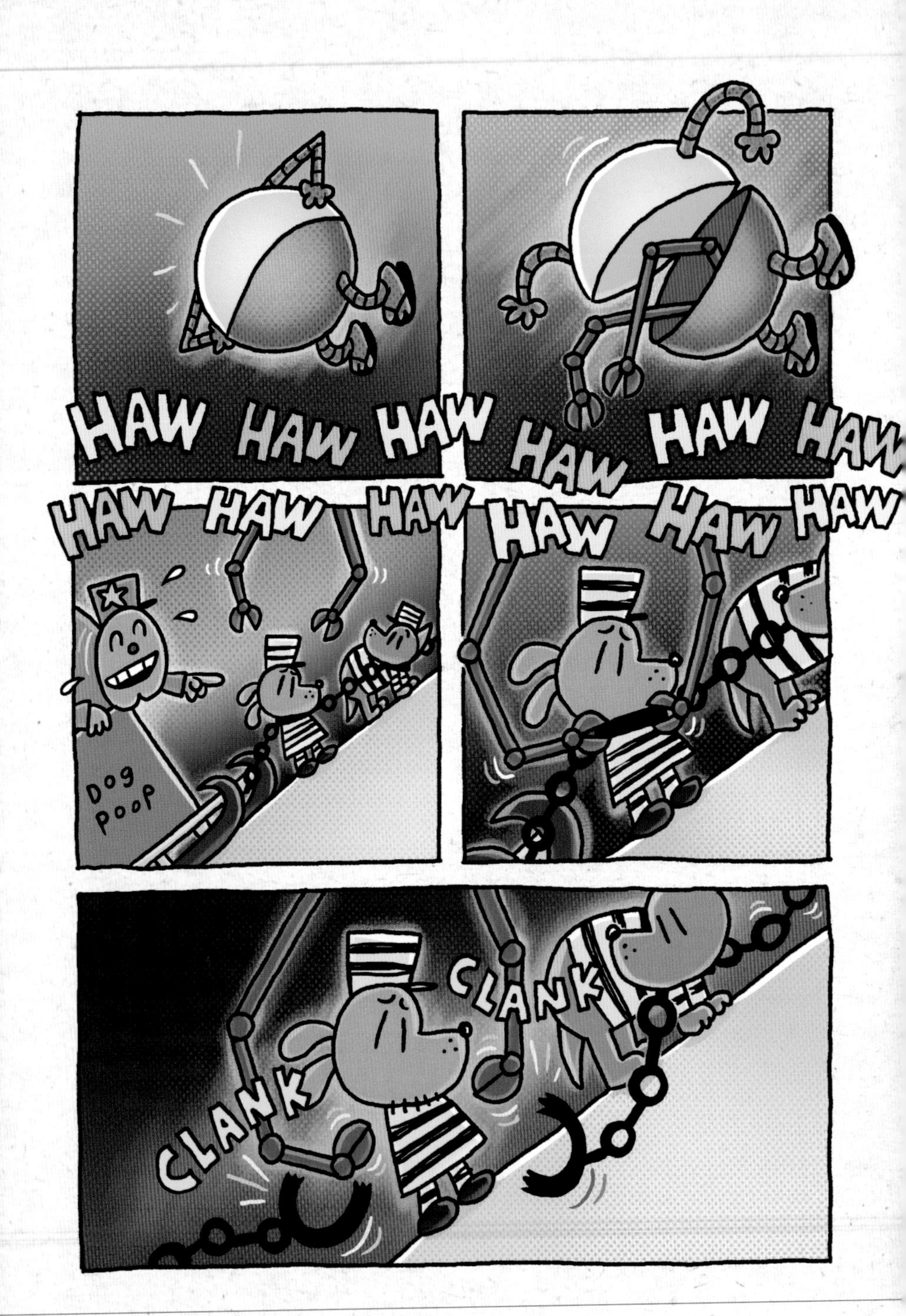
HAW HAW HAW HAW HAW HAW
HAW HAW HAW HAW HAW HAW
DOG POOP
CLANK
CLANK

But Then...
Tap
Tap
Tap

tap
Tap
tap

PUPPY YUM-YUMS

Shaka
Shaka
PUPPY YUM-YUMS
BEEFY Bones
Shaka
Shaka

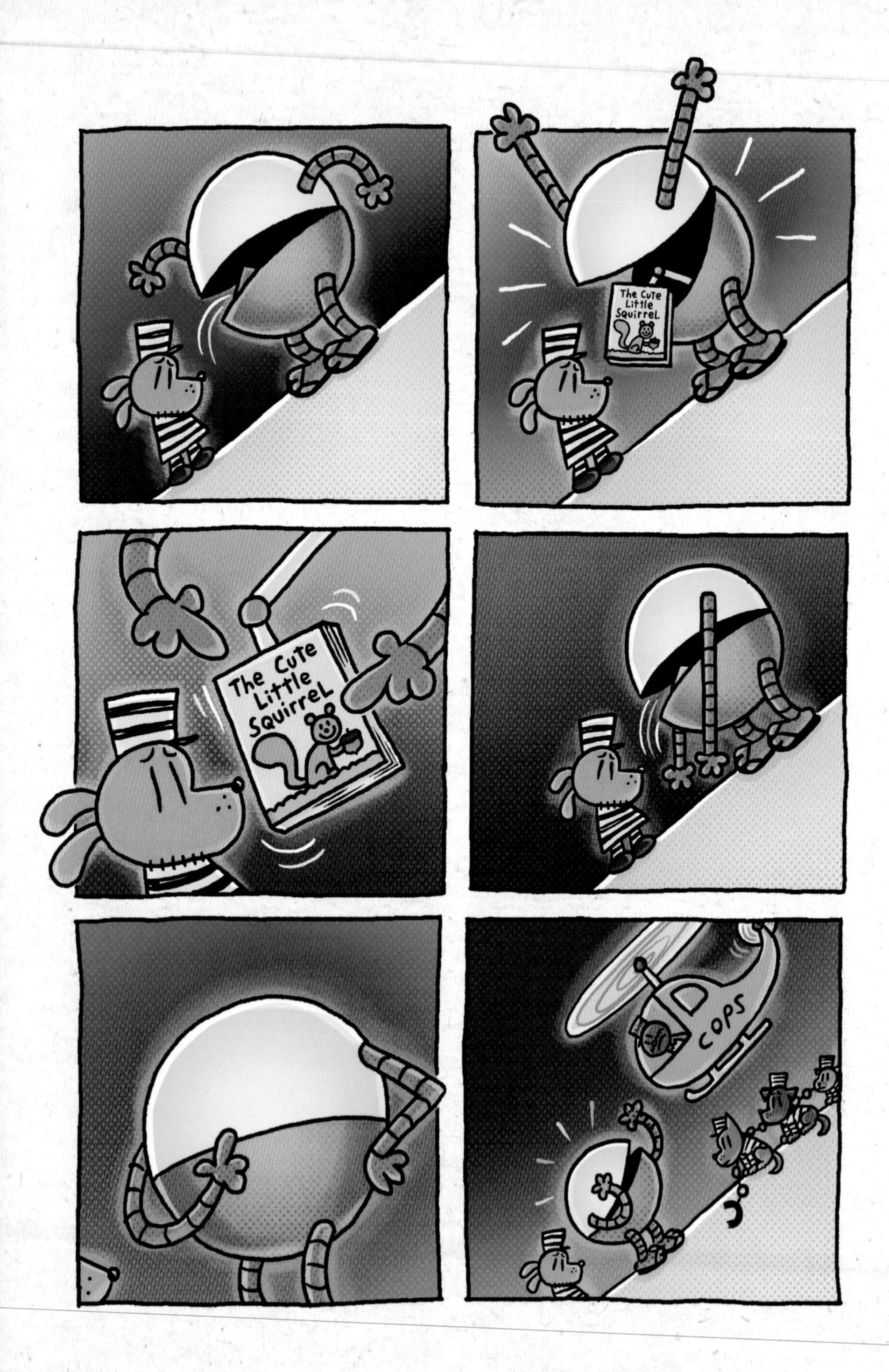
The Cute Little Squirrel
The Cute Little Squirrel
COPS

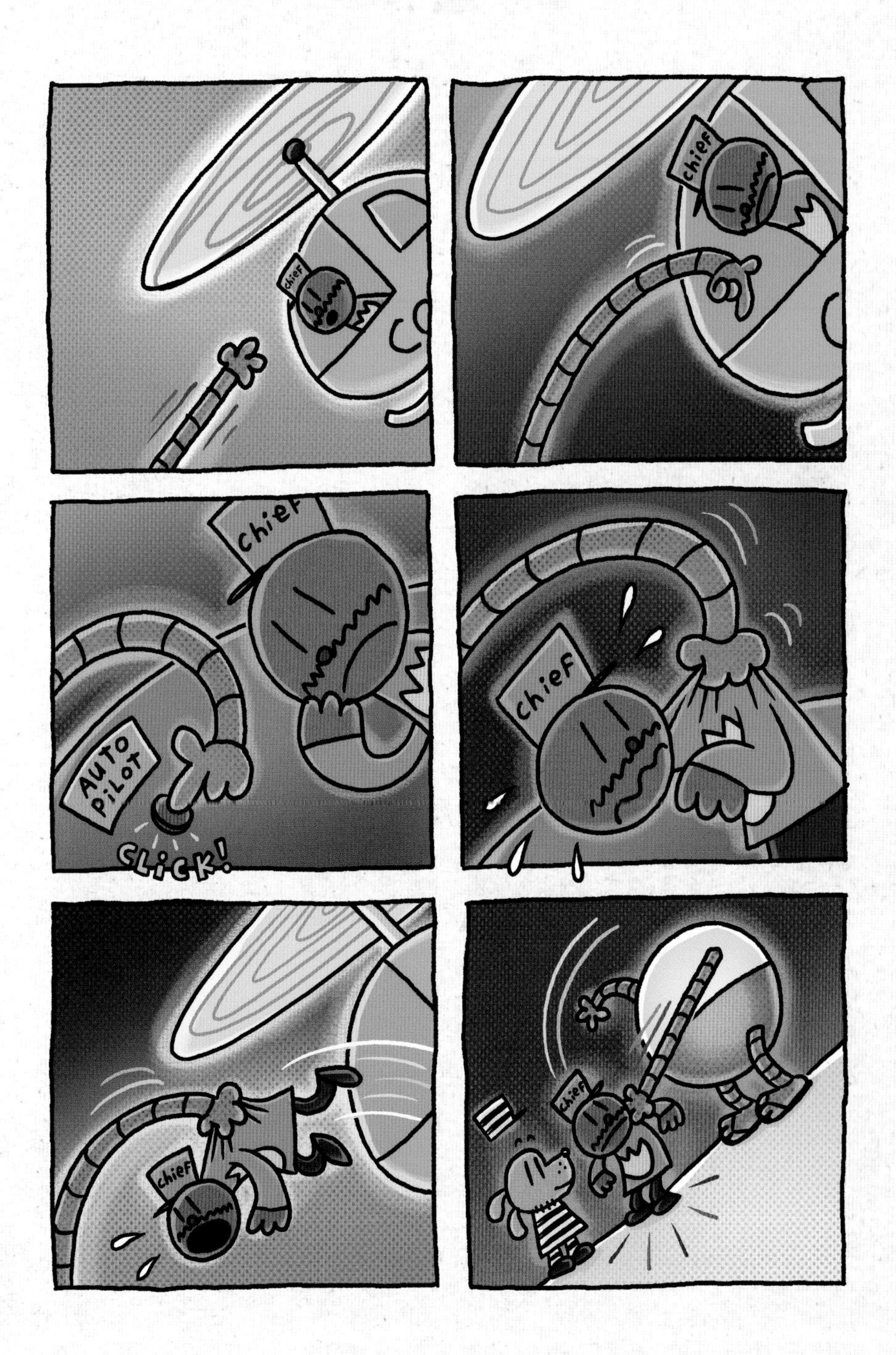
CHIEF
CHIEF
CHIEF
AUTO PILOT
CLICK!
CHIEF
CHIEF
CHIEF

Umm...
chief

...now wait Just a minute!!!
chief

chief
NO, WAiT!!!

NOOOOOO!!

STOP!

CUT iT OUT!!!

DOWN, BOY!

ENOUGH!

BAD DOGGY!

I mean...

Let's go home.

And so...
COPS
Climb aboard!
Chief

What's wrong, Dog Man?

What are you waiting for?

Forget those other dogs!
Chief

They were mean to you!!!
chief

They **GrowLed** at you!!!
chief

They turned their backs on you when you needed them most!!!
COPS
chief

But, Dog man...

We can't take all of these dogs with us!

They won't fit in the helicopter!!!
chief

chief

It's no use, 80-HD!
chief

He won't leave without them!
chief

chief

FLIP FLOP FLIP FLOP FLIP

chief

chief

chief

And so...
chief

chief

CLINK
CLANK
CLUNK
CLINK
CLANK
CLUNK

HAAAAK

SPIT-TOOIE!
chief

chief

Alright, gang, we don't have much time...
chief

If we hurry, we might make it back to the city...
CHIEF

...in time to watch the new Dog Man Movie!!!
COPS

LET'S GO!
CHIEF
COPS
DOG POOP

CHAPTER 9

DOG MAN
The MAJOR Motion Picture

Sam E. Hamilton Presents
A GASSY Behemoth Animation Production
DOG Man: The MAJOR Motion Picture
Featuring the vocal talents of: YoLay Caprese • Scooter McRibs
Ding-Dong Magoo • And Samson J. Johnson as "Chief"

soundtrack available on Gassy Behemoth 8-Tracks

K-9 Suitable for canines
Some material may be too intense for humans

Meanwhile...

HeY, Look! It's that Living Spray Factory Outlet over there!

And check it out: Somebody is robbing the place!
THAT Living Spray Factory outlet over There
we closed

Let's Get him!

STOP, YOU crazy impostor!

CRASH!

Now to find out who this impostor Really is!

HEY! It's those Little FLEAS guys from our last book!

That's Right! And we've got one final trick up our sleeve!!!

Living spray
Brings stuff to Life

FLIP
Living spray
Brings stuff to Life

OH, NO! They've got LIVING SPRAY!!!

If they spray it on that car, it'll COME TO LIFE!!!

And it'll be SUPA EVIL!!!

CHOMP

SWOOOSH

HEY! THAT POODLE STOLE MY LIVING SPRAY!!!

LEGGO MY LIVING SPRAY!

STAIRS
COPS
TONIGHT
DOG MAN
The MAJOR
MOTION PICTURE

BONK

C'mon, everybody!
chief

Let's go downstairs and watch the movie!
STAIRS
chief
COPS
TONIGHT

C'mon, Sarah!!! Let's go upstairs and save Zuzu!!!

FLIP FLOP
chief
Movie THeater

EXIT

GRAB
Living Spray
Brings Stuff To Life

HAW HAW HAW! We've got you Now!!!

Left
hand here.

Right
Thumb
here.

Hey, do you guys want some pop-corn?
chief

Thanks, Chief! Look, we caught the robber!
chief

It was just those little FLEAS guys in a robot suit!!
MOTOR OIL
chief

Hey! Where'd they go???
chief

Living
spray

Hurry up, Ya Lazy belly-scratchers!

And **I'm** Pressin' the button, too, so don't bother askin'!

SSSSS

SSSSSSSSSS

chief

chief
HELP!!!

Boy, this is the best 3-D Movie I've ever seen!
RUFF RUFF
RUFF RUFF

WARNING: CONTENTS
Under Pressure. Keep
away from flames
and stuff.

Stairs
D
COPS
TONIGHT
DOG MAN
The MAJOR
MOTION PICTURE

Stairs
D
COPS
TONIGHT
DOG MAN
KA-
BOOM!
BONK!

stairs
COPS
TONIGHT
DOG MAN
The MAJOR
MOTION PICTU

stairs
COPS
TONI
hT
The MAJOR
MOTION PIC

stairs
RUFF
RUFF
RUFF
COPS
TONIGHT
DOG MAN
The MAJOR
MOTION PICTURE

Meanwhile...
Cat Jail

Hey, Papa, when we finish fixing this bee...

...Can we go save Dog Man?
NO!

How come?
Why should I care About Dog Man?

He's the reason I got locked up in the first place!

Hey, Papa, do ya wanna hear a Joke?
CLICK

NO, I DON'T!
Why?

Because Your Jokes AREN'T FUNNY!
Why?

Because you Keep REPEATing Yourself!
Why?

BECAUSE YOU CAN'T KEEP DOING THE SAME DUMB THINGS OVER AND OVER AND OVER AGAIN!
Why?

Because if you're going to do some-thing, you should do it WELL!!!
Why?

Because you should try to IMPROVE!
Why?

Because if you don't challenge yourself to GROW, what's the POINT?
Why?

Because you should always strive to be a GREAT CAT!!!
Why?

HEY - I know what you're doing!

You're trying to TRICK ME!!!
why?

HOW SHOULD I KNOW?

Look here, Mister— I'm the BAD GUY!

That's All I've EVER BEEN!!!

You shouldn't keep repeating yourself, Papa.

You can't keep doing the same dumb things over and over again.

If you're going to do Something, you should do it well!

You should always try to improve!

Because if you don't challenge yourself to grow, what's the point?

You should always strive to be a GREAT CAT!

Right, Papa?

Chapter 10

The Great Cat's Bee

Live
Breaking News
We interrupt the beginning of this new chapter with a supa sensational news story!!!

Claymation Calamity
A clay monster guy came to life...

... and there's a big fire and a whole buncha other stuff!
Buncha other stuff...

Who will save us?
GAme over, man!

And So...
Cat Jail

There he is, Papa!

And he's got Chief!

ALright, hang on, Kid!

ZAP
POW
STAIRS
RUFF
RUFF RUFF

chief

You did it, Papa!!!
STAIRS

Yeah, well, if you want the job done right...

ULP!!!

80-HD, Don't fail me now!

FLIP FLOP FLIP FLOP

SNIP!

Stairs
chief
chief
WHAM

Why are you guys celebrating?

* Italian for: "Totally cheesed off!"

OK, you guys go Save the people...
chief

...and Dog Man and I will take care of Claymation Philly!

SHiNG
SHiNG

SWOOSH

BONK

Boing!

Boing
Boing

PLOP!

HEY!

Boing
HEY!

DANGER
Boing
Hey!

DANGER
RUMBLE
Rumble
Boing

CRASH

DOG MAN!

Dog Man?

MUNCH

Munch Munch
Munch

WAAAAA

WAAAAAA

WAAAAAAAAAAAAAAAAAAA
stairs
FLIP FLOP FLIP FLOP

TONIGHT
DOG MAN

We're too Late, 80-HD!

Dog Man got ate up by Claymation Philly!

While 80-HD worked to clear the boulders away from the cave...

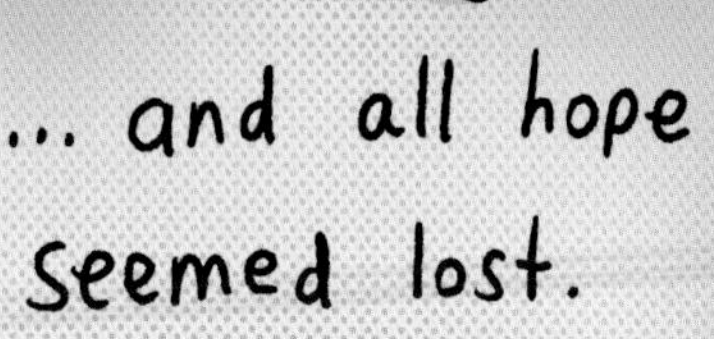

And we're stuck on this roof!!!
Stairs
chief

And somebody is still trapped in the theater!!!
Chief

And we can't get outta this hole!!!
Guard

And this sled is gonna CRASH!!!
Dog Poop
SCRAAPE!

And I'm almost out of Popcorn!!!

But then...

Hey! What's that?

OH, BOY! IT's DOG MAN!!! And he's ALive!!!

I thought Claymation Philly ate you up!!!

But you ate **him** up, didn't you?

Uh-oh! I think Dog Man's gonna hurl!!!

Hey, 80-HD! I got an idea!
whisper... whisper... whisper...

Left hand here.

Right Thumb here.

The

Dog Man barfed and barfed...

... until all the flames were put out.
TONIGHT

WOW! Dog Man's Voluminous Vomit saved us all!!!

Isn't that **Great?**

Chief

Soon, everyone was back safely on the ground.
HEY, LOOK!

Those dogs saved that guy who was trapped in the Theater!!!
BEST MOVIE EVER!

They're HEROES!
We should celebrate!

NOT SO FAST!

You guys think you're so smart!
Guard

But SOMEbody's gotta pay for what happened tonight!
Guard

I'll see you ALL in my COURT!
Guard

I'll be a witness against them!!!
OOOH!!! They're all gonna be SORRY!!!
Guard

You guys are gonna wish you were never, ever...
DOG POOP
SCRAAAAAPE!

HEY!
Food
Dog
Poop
BONK!

OH...
Dog
Poop

NOOOOOOOO
Dog
Poop

KLunk
BLUNK
KLank
Dog
Poop

FLiPPA
FLUMPA
FLOOPA
FRUNKA
FLOOPY
FLUP
Dog
Poop

Well, gang, it looks like we saved the world again!!!

Chapter 11

March of the Misfits

By George Beard and Harold Hutchins

Hey, Dog Man! Why are you sad?

I'll tell ya why he's sad.
chief

A buncha folks were mean to him today!!!
chief

They called him a **MISFIT**!!!
FLIP FLOP FLIP FLOP

Chief
Flop Flip Flop Flip Flop Flip Flop Flip

Don't feel bad, Dog Man.
Chief

I've never told anybody this...

...but I feel like a misfit, too.

HeY! So do I! Every day!!!
Chief

Grrr - Ruff - Ruff RRRUFF Ruff!!!

CLANK CLANK
CLANKiTy-CLANK

ZUZU and 80-HD said **They're** misfits, too!!!

The truth is, we're **ALL** misfits!

Even **YOU**, Yolay?
Heck yeah!!!

But you're so **PERFECT!!!**

I'm just ACTING! I only Pretend to be Perfect!

But deep down inside, I'm a Total Weirdo!
CHIEF

WOW! You had us all fooled!!!
Thanks!
CHIEF

Don't worry, Dog Man. Everybody feels like a misfit!!!

And that means you fit in...

... PerFecTLy!!!

And So...
Petey!
Cat Jail

It's good to have you back!!!

Let's play again Tomorrow, ok, Papa?
Sure, kid!

Hey, Papa?
Yeah?

Am I a misfit, too?

Are you kidding? You're the biggest misfit I've ever met!!!

Really?
Yup!

Sweeeeet!!!

The

End

●●●○○ UP&P LTE 11:30 PM 82%

pilkey.hatoffnews.com

Menu

SUPA BUDDIES SAVE THE DAY:

The Supa Buddies kept everybody safe during last night's tragic fire. Cat Kid, the leader of the Supa Buddies, was sad afterward because he forgot to sing their theme song (which he made up) during the big brawl. "Next time I'll remember better," said Cat Kid.

THE FLEAS: WHERE ARE THEY NOW?

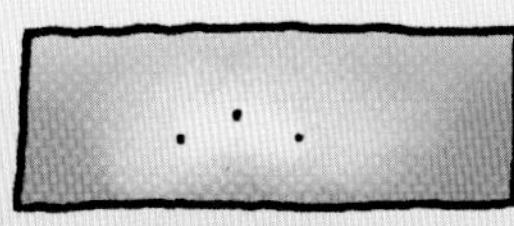

The FLEAS
(artist's depiction)

Nobody knows the whereabouts of Piggy, Crunky, and Bub (AKA The FLEAS). They were last seen in the burning movie theater, but then they disappeared.

"I just don't know what happened to them," said Petey the Cat as he scratched himself inside his jail cell this morning. "They just *vanished*," he continued, scratching again and again. "Where could they be?" he asked again, scratching vigorously

ey the Cat

●●●●○ UP&P LTE 11:31 PM 82%

pilkey.hatoffnews.com

Menu

HERO DOGS FIND FOREVER HOMES

The seven former inmates at Dog Jail were pardoned this morning for being heroes at last night's fire. They were immediately adopted by a buncha nice families and stuff, and are living happily ever after and stuff.

COMEUPPANCE

This morning, three meanies were pulled out of a stinky hole in the ground.
During the rescue, the rope broke and they fell back into the hole a buncha times.
It was awesome.

DOG MAN IS GO!

Reports are pouring in about an ALL-NEW Dog Man adventure that is coming your way. It will be available soon, but you should start bugging your parents, librarian, and/or bookseller about it now, just to be safe.
The title of this top secret book can now be revealed in this exclusive scoop:
The new book will be called DOG MA
!!! You heard it here first, folks!

CATKiD

in 49 Ridiculously easy steps!

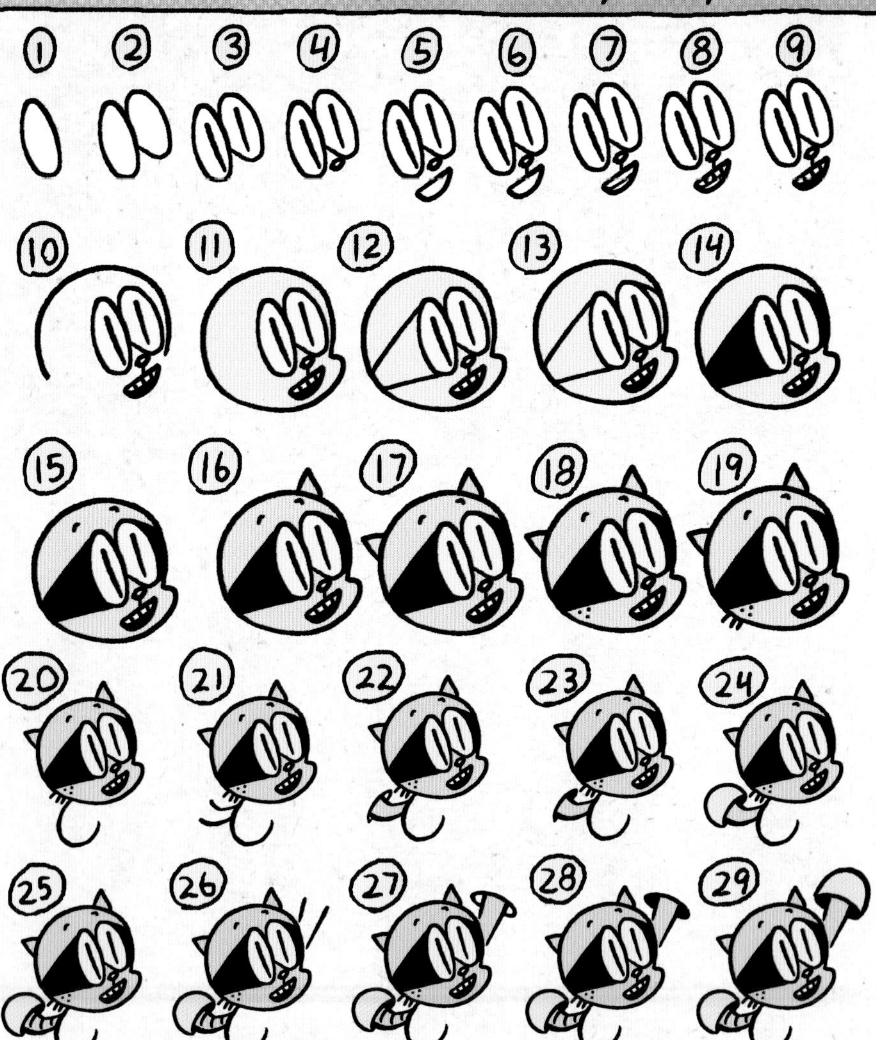

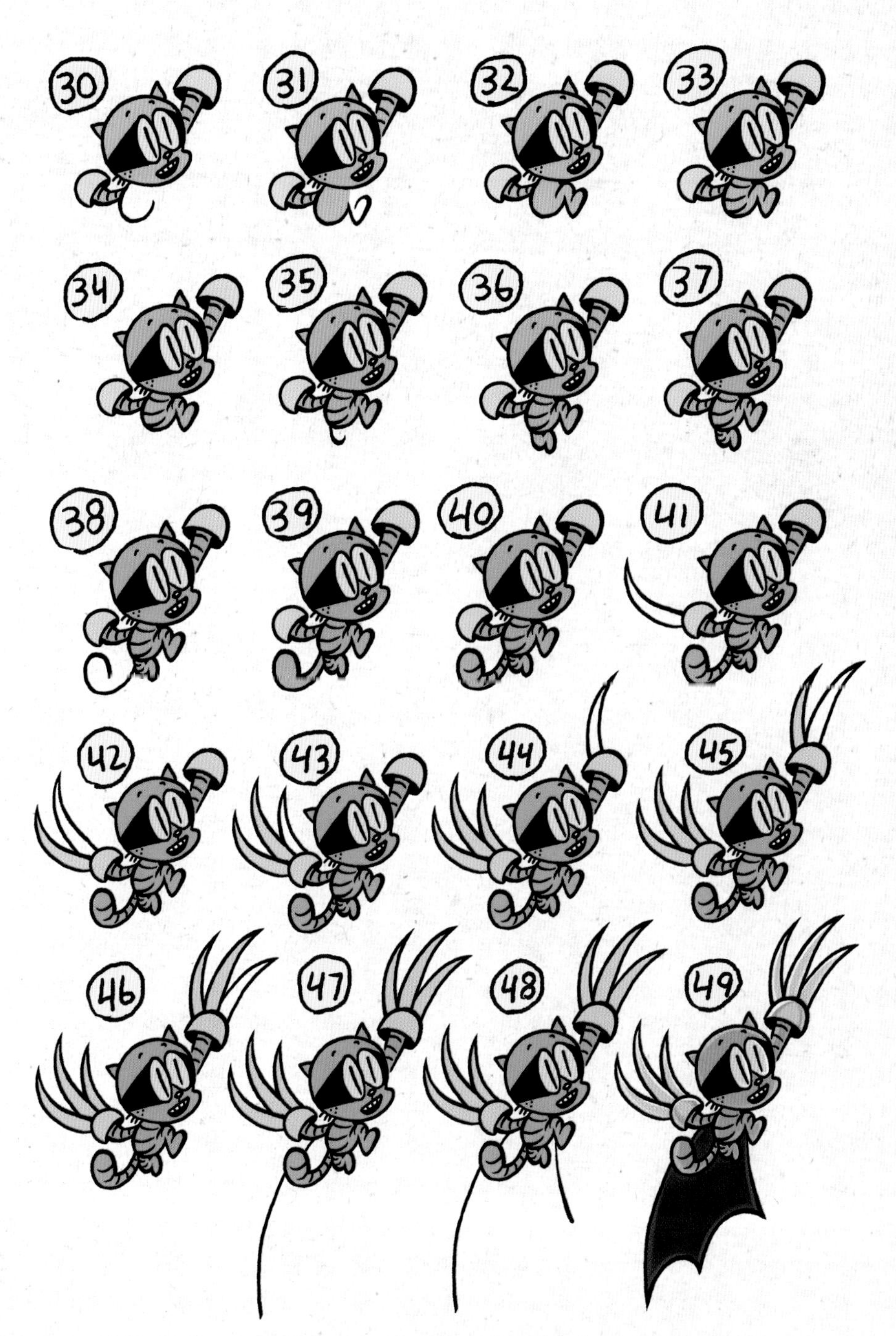
30
31
32
33
34
35
36
37
38
39
40
41
42
43
44
45
46
47
48
49

LIGHTNING DUDE

in 33 Ridiculously easy steps!

21
22
23
24
25
26
27
28
29
30
31
32
33

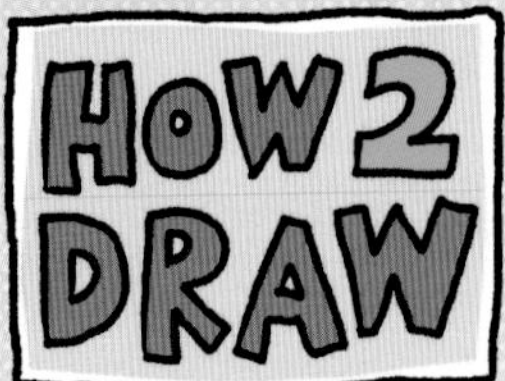

THE BARK KNIGHT

in 46 Ridiculously easy Steps!

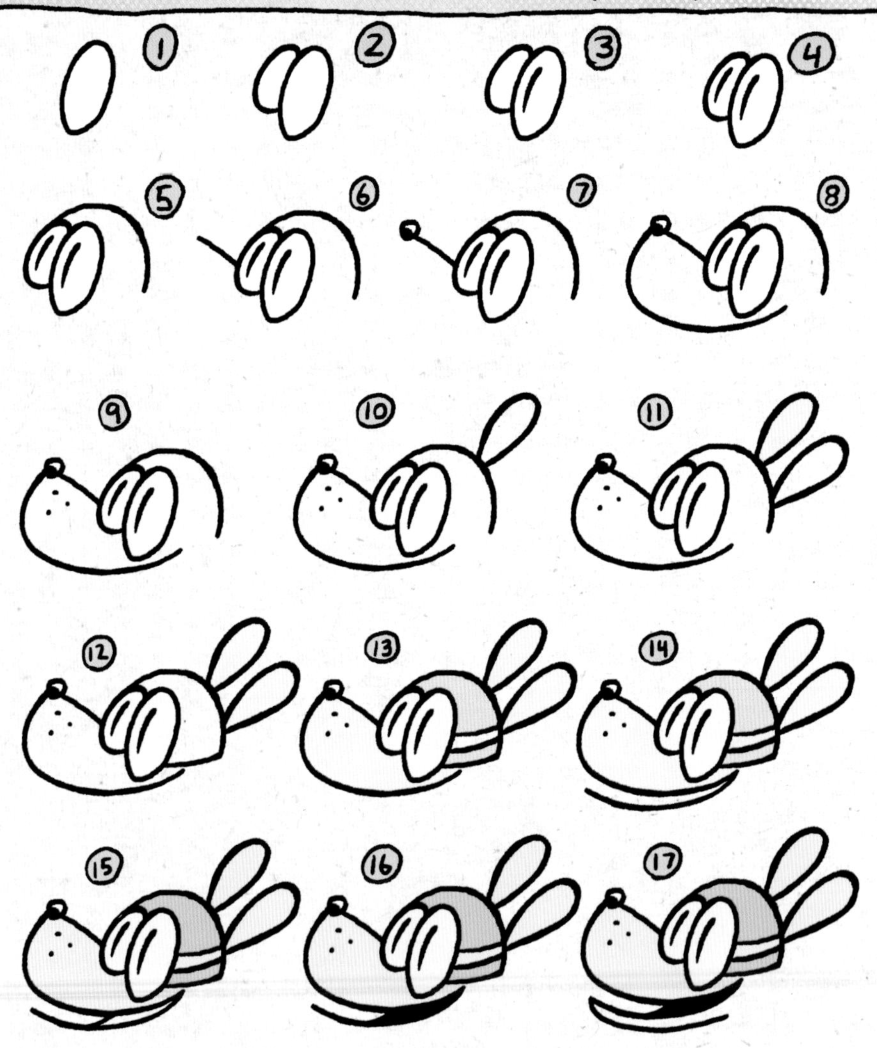

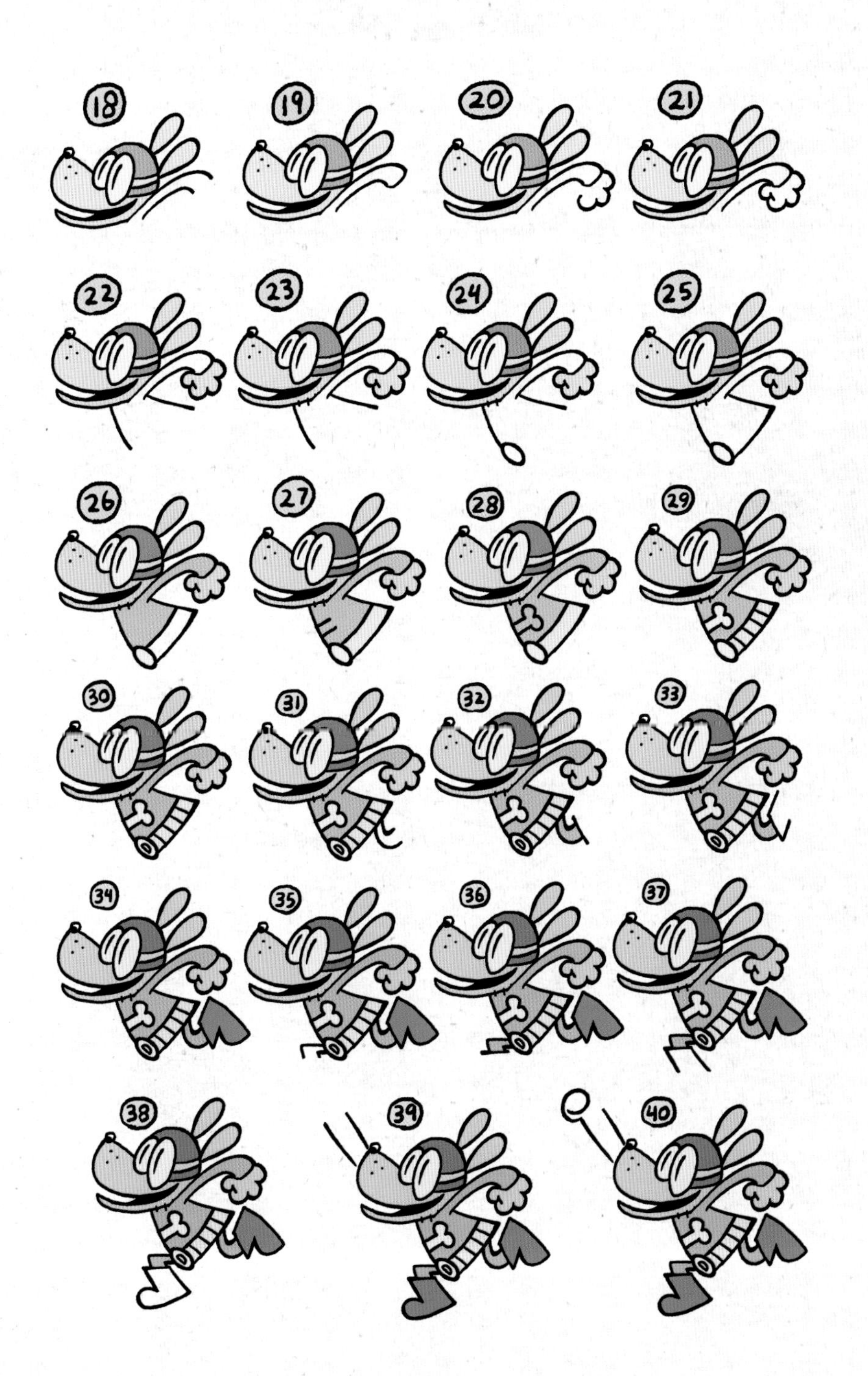
18
19
20
21
22
23
24
25
26
27
28
29
30
31
32
33
34
35
36
37
38
39
40

41
42
43
44
45
46

LEARN 2 DRAW MORE
STUFF!
at PLANETPILKEY.COM
chief

The FLEAS

in 3 Ridiculously easy steps!

① . ② .. ③ ...

BONUS SECTION

Learn to draw the FLEAS in these EXCITING NATURAL Habitats:

in a snowstorm

at night

in the fog

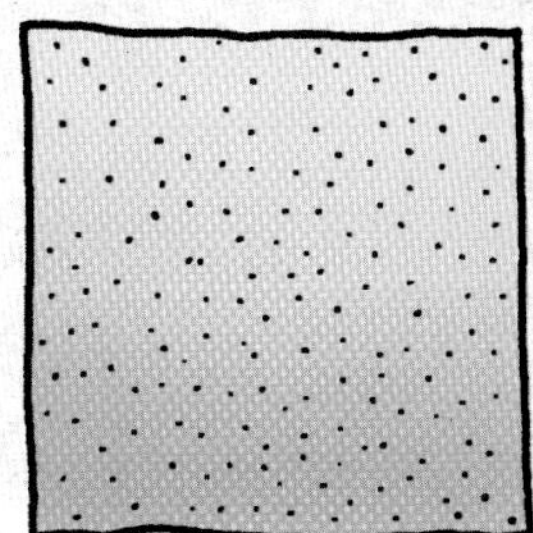
at the beach

in outer space

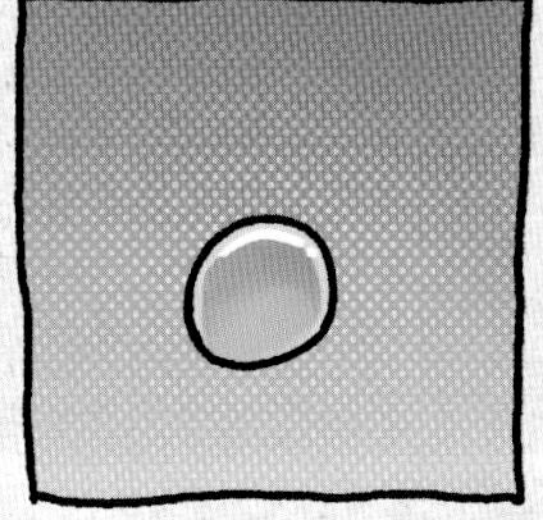
behind a grape

GET READING W

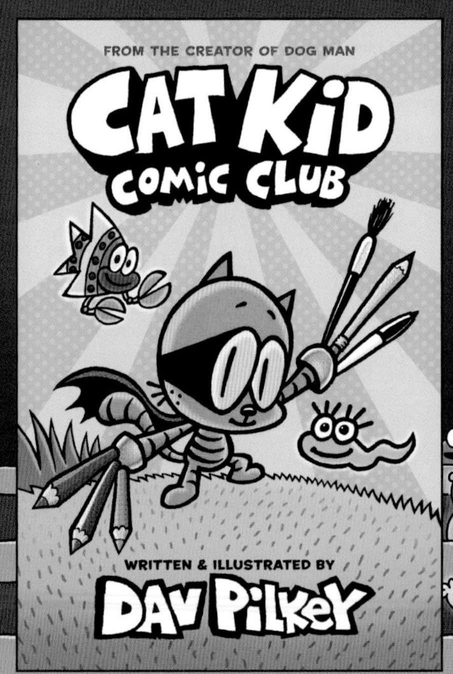

★ "Irreverent, laugh-out-loud funny, and . . . downright moving."
— Publishers Weekly, starred review